STORY AND ART BY

NORIYUKI KONISHI

ORIGINAL CONCEPT AND SUPERVISED BY LEVEL-5 INC.

YO-KAI WATCH™

Volume 17

VIZ Media Edition

Story and Art by Noriyuki Konishi
Original Concept and Supervised by LEVEL-5 Inc.

Translation/Tetsuichiro Miyaki
English Adaptation/Aubrey Sitterson
Lettering/John Hunt
Design/Kam Li
Editor/Megan Bates

YO-KAI WATCH Vol. 17
by Noriyuki KONISHI

Printed in the U.S.A.

Published by VIZ Media, LLC
P.O. Box 77010
San Francisco, CA 94107

10 9 8 7 6 5 4 3 2 1
First printing, May 2021

YO-KAI WATCH™
17
STORY AND ART BY
NORIYUKI KONISHI
ORIGINAL CONCEPT AND SUPERVISED BY LEVEL-5 INC.

CHARACTER INTRODUCTION

NATE ADAMS

AN ORDINARY ELEMENTARY SCHOOL STUDENT. WHISPER GAVE HIM THE YO-KAI WATCH AND HE'S USED IT TO MAKE A BUNCH OF YO-KAI FRIENDS!

WHISPER

A YO-KAI BUTLER FREED BY NATE, WHISPER USES HIS EXTENSIVE KNOWLEDGE TO TEACH HIM ALL ABOUT YO-KAI!

JIBANYAN

A CAT WHO BECAME A YO-KAI WHEN HE PASSED AWAY. HE IS FRIENDLY, CAREFREE, AND THE FIRST YO-KAI THAT NATE BEFRIENDED. HE'S BEEN TRYING TO FIGHT TRUCKS, BUT HE ALWAYS LOSES.

WHISPER
A FUTURE FORM OF THE YO-KAI WHISPER.
TATE ADAMS
NATE'S SON WHO DREAMS OF BECOMING A HERO.
JIBANYAN
A FUTURE FORM OF THE YO-KAI JIBANYAN.
JACK COBBLER
A BOY FROM 60 YEARS AGO WHO FOUGHT IN A BATTLE TO SAVE THE YO-KAI WORLD WITH GUSTO.
HOVERNYAN
A HOVERING CAT YO-KAI WHO CAN TRAVEL THROUGH TIME.
GUSTO
A COMPASSIONATE CLASSIC YO-KAI WHO IS JACK'S FRIEND.

TABLE OF CONTENTS

CHAPTER 164: INNOCENT YO-KAI SNOW SPECT-HARE

WHAT DO YOU MEAN? IT'S SNOWING OUTSIDE...
...SO I FLUFFED UP MY FUR TO KEEP WARM!
ROLL ROLL...
I SEE...
BUT I'M TIRED OF LYING AROUND! LET'S GO OUTSIDE AND HAVE A SNOWBALL FIGHT!
WOOHOO!
LET'S GO, NATE!

NAH, IT'S TOO COLD.
...
HE'S RIGHT.
ROLL ROLL...
OH... ALL RIGHT THEN!
...
...
...
WAITA-MINUTE! THIS STORY ISN'T GOING ANYWHERE! WE'VE GOT TO DO SOME-THING!
WHAT ABOUT ALL THIS SNOW?! LET'S DO A CHAPTER THAT WOULDN'T BE POSSIBLE DURING THE SUMMERTIME!
WE'VE ALREADY USED THREE PAGES, SO WE DON'T HAVE MUCH SPACE LEFT!
...
JIBANYAN'S RIGHT! WE SHOULD TAKE ADVANTAGE OF THIS WEATHER!
LET'S GO PLAY IN THE SNOW!
YEAH!♪

FWOOOOO
SHUDDER
SHUDDER
SHUDDER
SHUDDER
TRRMBLE
TRRMBLE
TRRMBLE
TRRMBLE
TRRMBLE
TRRMBLE
IT'S FREEZ-ING!
LET'S GO HOME!
PLEASE!
ZUFF
I HAD IT ALL WRONG!
ONLY MANGA SERIES THAT HAVE RUN OUT OF IDEAS DO CHAPTERS BASED ON SEASONS!
I DIDN'T KNOW IT'D BE SO COLD!! I'M SO SORRY!!
?
HE'S BEING SO SINCERE...
BUT I KNOW WHAT HE'S DOING. HE'S GOING TO MAKE A JOKE ON THE NEXT PAGE.
YUP.

I MEANT NO HARM WHEN I PROPOSED A WINTER-THEMED CHAPTER, BUT I APOLOGIZE FROM THE BOTTOM OF MY HEART FOR WASTING ALL OF THESE PAGES!
OH, I SEE... HE'S GOING TO APOLOGIZE A LITTLE MORE BEFORE HE TURNS IT INTO A JOKE.
LOOKS LIKE IT.
NO! IT'S NOTHING LIKE THAT!
I'M GIVING YOU A SINCERE APOLOGY RIGHT NOW!
HE SOUNDS SERIOUS.
OH! **ACTUALLY,** IT'S...
YUP.
...A YO-KAI.
MM-HMM.
!
TRRMBLE TRRMBLE
AH-HA! I SEE YOU HAVE A YO-KAI WATCH! ♪
I WAS WONDERING HOW YOU WERE TALKING TO A YO-KAI!

FWUMP FWUMP FWUMP
HELLO, HELLO! ♪
IT'S A WALKING, TALKING SNOWMAN!
A snowman Yo-kai?!
EEK!
WHOOPS! I COMPLETELY FORGOT I WAS PLAYING SNOWMAN BY MYSELF!
WHAT? WHO TURNS THEMSELVES INTO A SNOWMAN?!
THUNGK THUNGK THUNGK
STUPID, STUPID, STUPID, STUPID!
...

I'M SO SORRY FOR STARTLING YOU!
I'M SORRY! REALLY, TRULY SORRY!
IT'S OKAY, REALLY. WHAT ARE YOU, A BEGGING-FOR-FORGIVENESS YO-KAI?
IT'S... OKAY?
THANK YOU SO VERY MUCH! YOU'RE SO NICE!
!
GLOMP
SHA
WHOA! YOUR HANDS ARE SO COLD!
!

I'M SORRY! I FORGOT THAT MY BODY WAS MADE OF SNOW!
I'M SO SORRY FOR BEING SO COLD! I REALLY APOLOGIZE!
HUFF HUFF
YOU'RE MADE OF SNOW? WOW...
THIS IS—
SNOW SPECT-HARE.
AN INNOCENT YO-KAI WITH A HEART AS WHITE AS SNOW!
INNOCENT YO-KAI SNOW SPECT-HARE
INNOCENT, HUH? IS THAT WHY SHE APOLOGIZES THE SECOND SHE THINKS SHE'S DONE SOMETHING WRONG?
SO WHEN YOU'RE INSPIRITED BY HER, SHE MAKES YOU INNOCENT!
THAT'S WHY JIBANYAN WAS APOLOGIZING SO MUCH!
...
IT MIGHT SEEM LIKE THAT, BUT...

I'M NOT EVEN INTER-ESTED IN INSPIRITING PEOPLE. ♪
I JUST LIKE WATCHING PEOPLE HAVE FUN PLAYING IN THE SNOW! ♪
HMM, I DIDN'T KNOW THERE WERE YO-KAI LIKE THAT...
WHAT?! THAT'S NOT HOW A YO-KAI IS SUPPOSED TO ACT!
YO-KAI ARE SUPPOSED TO INSPIRIT PEOPLE AND HELP THEM!
SOME OF THEM END UP CAUSING TROUBLE, BUT INSPIRITING IS WHAT YO-KAI ARE ALL ABOUT!
BUT...YOU DON'T INSPIRIT ANYONE. YOU JUST GET HIT BY TRUCKS.
?!
HE'S RIGHT.
HOW RUDE! WHAT DO YOU MEAN, I JUST GET HIT BY TRUCKS?!
I—
...
I...
THUNK
...

I'M A FAILURE AS A YO-KAI!
COME ON NOW, YOU'RE NOT THAT BAD. ♪
WHISPER DOESN'T INSPIRIT ANYONE EITHER ...
DON'T WORRY! ♪ PEOPLE DON'T REALLY CARE WHAT YO-KAI DO THESE DAYS. ♪
?
YOU'RE RIGHT!

AS LONG AS YOUR NAME'S A PUN, THAT'S MORE THAN ENOUGH. ♪
HEY! DON'T TELL THEM THAT!
AH!
I'M SORRY! I WAS BEING TOO HONEST!
STOP! SAYING YOU WERE BEING HONEST MAKES IT EVEN WORSE!
...
RRMBL...

YOU'RE RIGHT!
THUNGK THUNGK
I'M SO SORRY! STUPID, STUPID, STUPID!
HEY! HEY!
KRRRRRRK
AIYEEEEEE!
HEEEEEEY!
SHE'S MADE OF SNOW.

YOU'RE BEING TOO APOLOGETIC.
PAPT
PAPT
I'M SORRY ...
ALL RIGHT, YOU! I'VE HAD ENOUGH!
SHE REMADE HERSELF WITH FRESH SNOW.
JUST BECAUSE YOU'RE INNOCENT DOESN'T GIVE YOU THE RIGHT TO DO WHATEVER YOU WANT!
HE'S RIGHT! YOU MUST THINK YOU CAN GET AWAY WITH ANYTHING AS LONG AS YOU APOLOGIZE ...
THAT'S NOT ...
NO! I'M ANGRY BECAUSE...
?
...I'M ONE OF THE MAIN CHARACTERS BUT YOU'VE BEEN GET-TING ALL THE ATTENTION WITH YOUR JOKES!!
IT'S NOT FAIR! EEEEK! MEEOOW!
BUT YOU'RE NOT DOING ANYTHING BAD, SO I CAN'T EVEN PUNCH YOU!
WOULD YOU CALM DOWN?
SHUT UP!!
TUMP TUMP TUMP TUMP
THAT'S YOUR PROBLEM ?
I'M SO SORRY! I PROMISE I DIDN'T MEAN TO!
GLOMP
I'M SORRY I MADE YOU FEEL BAD!
...
WOW!! YOU CALMED JIBAN-YAN DOWN SO QUICKLY!

I'M SORR ...
HUH?
M-MEOW ...
KRRKT
HE'S NOT CALM! HE'S FROZEN SOLID BECAUSE SHE HELD HIS HANDS!
I'M SO SORRY! I FORGOT I WAS MADE OF SNOW!
THUNGK THUNGK THUNGK
STUPID, STUPID, STUPID!
...
KRRRRRK
AIYEEEEEE!
ENOUGH ALREADY !!

HEH HEH HEH... I GUESS I LOSE.
!
SHE MADE A NEW HEAD.
I WAS NO MATCH FOR HER...
I'D LIKE TO APOLOGIZE TO ALL THE READERS WHO WERE EXPECTING THAT I WOULD TAKE A MORE ACTIVE ROLE.
I'M SORRY TO DISAP-POINT YOU.
HE'S BEING APOLOGETIC AGAIN...
IT MUST BE SNOW SPECT-HARE'S INFLU-ENCE.
I HAVEN'T DONE ANYTHING.
WHAT?

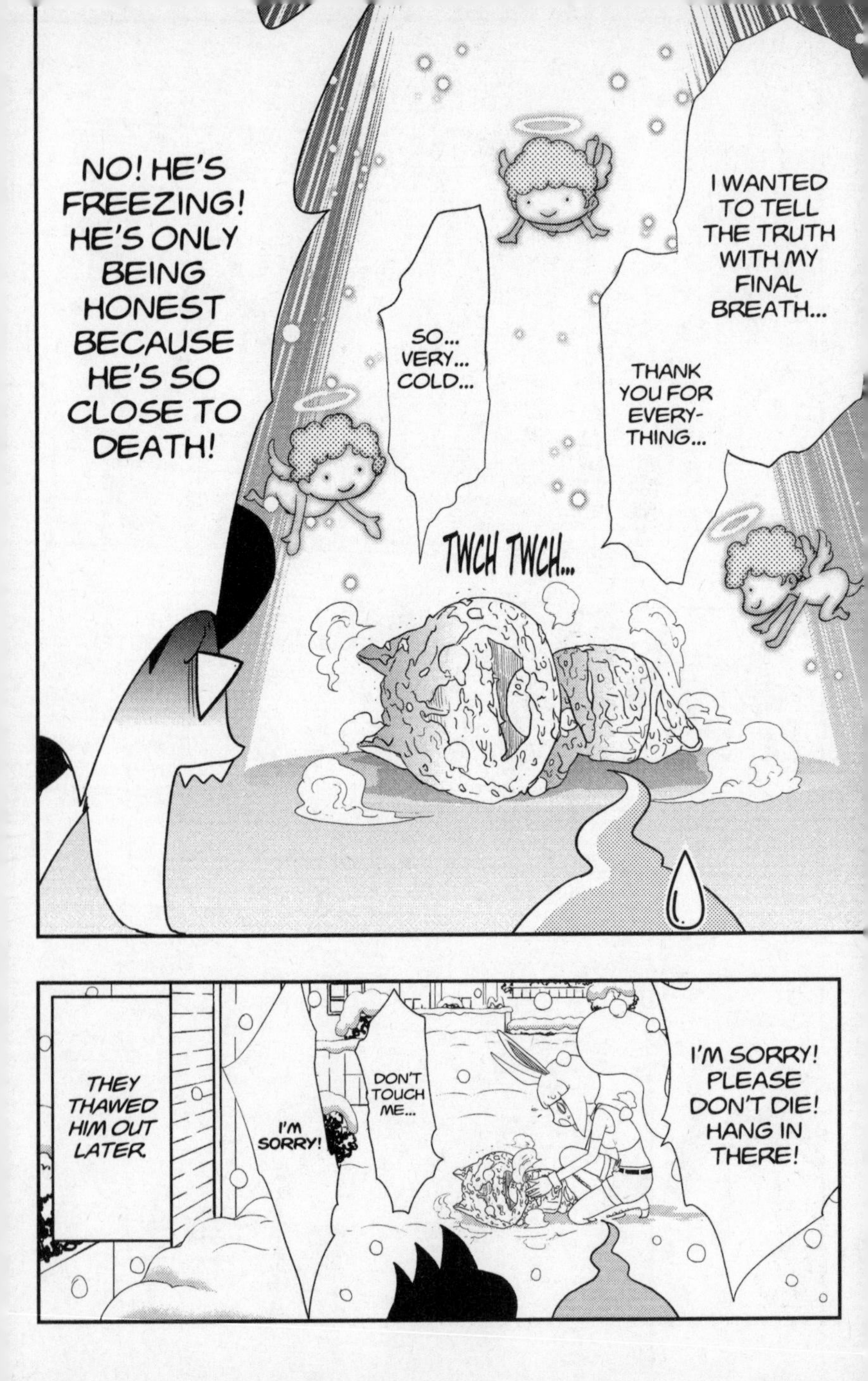
I WANTED TO TELL THE TRUTH WITH MY FINAL BREATH...
THANK YOU FOR EVERY-THING...
SO... VERY... COLD...
NO! HE'S FREEZING! HE'S ONLY BEING HONEST BECAUSE HE'S SO CLOSE TO DEATH!
TWCH TWCH...
I'M SORRY! PLEASE DON'T DIE! HANG IN THERE!
DON'T TOUCH ME...
I'M SORRY!
THEY THAWED HIM OUT LATER.

CHAPTER 165:
QUESTION YO-KAI
WHY NAANT
NNNGHH
TWCH
TWCH
VRRROOM...
HUUNH?
...

BAAM
WHAT ?!
...
WHYYYY?
CHOMP CHOMP CHOMP
I'VE BEEN WATCHING YOU... WHY DO YOU KEEP TRYING TO FIGHT TRUCKS EVERY DAY?
MNCH MNCH MNCH...
WHAT ?!
WHY NAANT?
I WAS HIT BY ONE AND DIED.
IT MADE THE GIRL I BELONGED TO SAD, SO I WANT TO BECOME A CAT WHO WON'T BE DEFEATED BY VEHICLES!
...

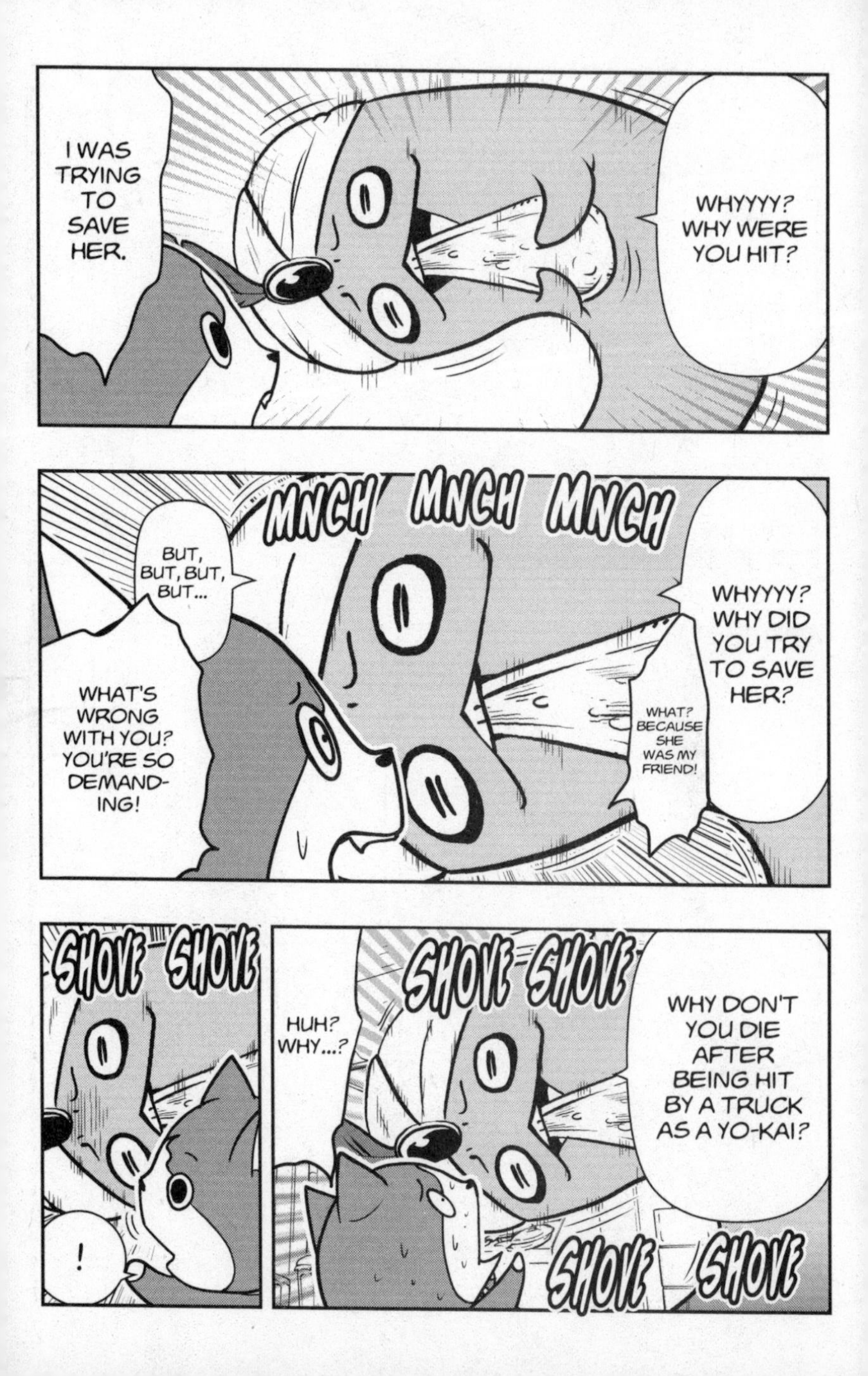
WHYYYY? WHY WERE YOU HIT?
I WAS TRYING TO SAVE HER.
MNCH MNCH MNCH
WHYYYY? WHY DID YOU TRY TO SAVE HER?
WHAT? BECAUSE SHE WAS MY FRIEND!
BUT, BUT, BUT, BUT...
WHAT'S WRONG WITH YOU? YOU'RE SO DEMAND-ING!
SHOVE SHOVE
WHY DON'T YOU DIE AFTER BEING HIT BY A TRUCK AS A YO-KAI?
HUH? WHY...?
SHOVE SHOVE
SHOVE SHOVE
!

AGGGH!
THUNGK!
SHA
W-WHY...
TWCH TWCH TWCH...
DO YOU GET IT NOW? I DON'T DIE BECAUSE I'M LUCKY.
WHA...
FWUMP
...
FWOOOO
HE DIED!
QUESTION YO-KAI WHY NAANT

WHYYYY?! WHY DIDN'T YOU TELL ME A TRUCK WAS COMING?
THIS IS NO TIME TO BE ASKING ME WHY! YOU JUST DIED!
FWOO FWOO
...
FWOO
FWOO
SHUP
SHFF
FWIP
SOOOO... WHY?
WHAT?! YOU JUST CAME BACK TO LIFE SOME-HOW?!
WHYYYY?!
...

W-W-W-W-WHYYYY ?!
CHOOM
CHOOM
CHOOM
SHUT UP!
CHOOM
CHOOM
CHOOM
RRMBELL...
WHY ...
RRMBELL...
DID MY PAWS OF FURY NOT WORK ?!
WHYYYY? WHY DID YOU PUNCH ME?

NNNNNGH
WHYYYYY?!
NO! IT WORKED PERFECT-LY!
WHY DID YOU PUNCH ME?! WHY? WHYYYY?
BECAUSE YOU'RE BEING OBNOX-IOUS!
...

BAAM
I SEE.
Everyone says that.
PAP
YOU'RE SATISFIED BY THAT ANSWER ?!
WHAAAAA?!
WHYYYY? WHY DIDN'T YOU THINK I'D BE SATISFIED WITH THAT ANSWER?
Mnch, mnch, mnch
HEY! HEY! HEY! WHY? WHYYYY?
ENOUGH!
IF YOU REALLY WANT TO KNOW, IT'S WHY NAANT'S FAULT!

CHAPTER 166:
MASCOT YO-KAI
HARRY BARRY
THE FISH PLACE
I'M HARRY BARRY, THE OFFICIAL MASCOT OF HARRISVILLE! ♪
I'M HERE TO PROMOTE HARRISVILLE! ♪
MASCOT YO-KAI HARRY BARRY
SHF SHF SHF
BUT EVERYONE'S IGNORING ME!
OF COURSE THEY ARE! YO-KAI ARE INVISIBLE TO HUMANS!
SHF SHF SHF SHF
OH, I SEE! ♪
WAIT...

GLOOOM
WHY DID I EVEN BOTHER COMING HERE?!
RRMMBBLL
I HAVE NO OTHER CHOICE...
I'LL JUST GO SIGHTSEEING AND THEN HEAD HOME! ♪
TRALALA ♪
WHAAAAAT!?
HE GAVE UP ALREADY?!
HOW COULD HE ABANDON HIS DUTY?! HE'S TURNED AWAY FROM HIS DESTINY!

I'LL NEVER GIVE UP ON MY DREAM! I'LL BEAT THIS TRUCK AND BE REUNITED WITH AMY!
VISH
PAWS OF FURY!
HEY!
GET OUT OF THE WAY!
THUN GKT
URGGHHH!

AIYEEE!
WHOOPS!
THUNGKT
ZSSSH
URRGH...
NNNNNGH
!
TUMP
YOU LEAPT RIGHT IN FRONT OF THAT TRUCK!
WHAT WERE YOU THINKING?!

YOU CAN'T ABANDON YOUR DUTY! YOU MUST NOT TURN AWAY FROM YOUR DESTINY!
YOU WERE BORN FOR A REASON! NEVER GIVE UP ON YOUR DREAM!
WAIT ...
?
ALL THIS FROM A GUY WHO ABAN-DONED HIS DUTY TO GO SIGHT-SEEING?!
HMM ...
WHAT IS MY DUTY?
DUUUH!
YOU ALREADY FORGOT?!
WELL, ANY-WAY ...
RRMMBLL

YOU'VE GOT QUITE A PUNCH ...
UGGH
I WENT OVER-BOARD. I'M SORRY.
I THOUGHT YOU WERE GIVING UP ON YOUR DESTINY!
NO WAY! I WAS JUST TRAINING TO GET STRONGER.
BUT YOU'RE SO STRONG. I BET YOU'LL MAKE A GREAT TRAINING PARTNER!
SPAR WITH ME BEFORE YOU GO SIGHT-SEEING!
!!!

PAWS OF FURY!
YOU'D DARE ATTACK THE YO-KAI WHO JUST SAVED YOUR LIFE?!
I REFUSE...
...TO TAKE PART IN...
...MEAN-INGLESS BATTLES!
HUFH
HUFH
WHAT'S THIS GUY'S DEAL? HE'S INCREDIBLY STRONG...

HNNRRGH
ALL MY PUNCHES LANDED!
...BUT HIS DEFENSE STINKS!
YOU GOT ME...
I DON'T LIKE FIGHT-ING.
STAGGER...
I'M SORRY... YOU'RE SO STRONG, I THOUGHT YOU COULD TAKE IT.
HOW ABOUT I GIVE YOU A TOUR TO APOLOGIZE?
WHERE WOULD YOU LIKE TO GO FIRST?
HOW ABOUT...THE HOSPITAL...?
TWCH TWCH...
HNNGH
...
IF YOU FORGET WHAT YOU'RE MEANT TO DO, IT MIGHT BE BECAUSE OF HARRY BARRY!

CHAPTER 167: DARK HERO KAPED KOMANDER

NO ONE'S HERE...

SHFF...

SHK
SHFF
THERE'S SO MUCH GARBAGE! CLEANING UP'S GOING TO BE A BLAST! ♪
DASH
!!!
YOU! WITH THE MASK! YOU LOOK SUSPI-CIOUS!
MEOW?!
GLARE
!!!

...
SWIP
KLAK
GOT IT! ♪
YOU'RE PICKING UP TRASH?! WHO ARE YOU?!
I'M A DARK HERO WHO DOES GOOD DEEDS BEHIND PEOPLE'S BACKS.
FIDGET FIDGET...
DARK HERO KAPED KOMANDER
ARE YOU EMBARRASSED TO BE CALLED A HERO OR SOMETHING?
IF YOU DO SOMETHING GOOD YOU SHOULD BE PROUD OF IT!
NO, I'M EMBARRASSED TO DO GOOD DEEDS IN FRONT OF OTHER PEOPLE...
FIDGET FIDGET TMP TMP
...
HEY, THAT'S GREAT! SO MANY PEOPLE TRY TO SHOW OFF THEIR ACHIEVEMENTS!
AWW, YOU'RE TOO KIND. ♪
PLIP
PLIP
?

FISH
PLIP
PLIP
YO-KAI KAPED KOMANDER ON THE JOB!
KAPED KOMANDER CLEANED UP ALL THE TRASH BY HIMSELF WITHOUT TELLING ANYONE ABOUT IT! THAT'S HIS SECRET!
DARK HERO KAPED KOMANDER
WHAT?! YOU'RE JUST USING NOTES TO SHOW OFF INSTEAD!
HEY! WHO ARE YOU ANYWAY?! WHAT ARE YOU DOING OUT RIGHT NOW?!
YOU LOOK SUSPI-CIOUS!
...
ISH
SH PLACE
TRAINING TO BEAT VEHICLES ...?
ACTUALLY, I...

WAAAAAH!
YOU TRIED TO PROTECT YOUR OWNER FROM A TRUCK BUT IT HIT YOU! SO NOW YOU FIGHT TRUCKS BECAUSE YOU'RE ASHAMED OF YOURSELF!
TOUCHED
WAAAAAH!
PLUS, YOU'RE ASHAMED OF MAKING HER SAD BY DYING! YOU'RE INCREDIBLE!
YOU CAN DO IT!
THANK YOU.
HOW-EVER ...

HOW DARE YOU ATTACK AN INNOCENT TRUCK!
YOU FIEND!
AS A HERO, I CANNOT FORGIVE YOU!
WHAAAAAT?! BUT YOU JUST SAID HOW TOUCHED YOU WERE!
SHOOOCK
THAT'S IRRELEVANT!
AS A HERO, I CAN'T ALLOW YOU TO CAUSE TROUBLE!
YOU MUST PRO-MISE TO STOP FIGHT-ING TRUCKS!
...

BAM
SO STAY OUT OF MY WAY!
I HAVE TO BECOME STRONG ENOUGH TO BEAT A TRUCK. I MUST KEEP TRAINING!
I'M SORRY ...
FINE! I'LL JUST HAVE TO DEFEAT YOU TO PROTECT ALL THE INNOCENT TRUCKS OUT THERE!
YOU'VE GIVEN ME NO OTHER CHOICE ...!
THE BEST FRE
SHAA

THUNGKT
VRRROOM
AHHHH!
...

NNNGH... FIENDISH TRUCKS... AVENGE ME...!
TWCH TWCH...
VRROOM
YOU CHANGED YOUR TUNE PRETTY QUICK...
WHEN YOU'RE EMBAR-RASSED ABOUT DOING SOMETHING GOOD, MAYBE KAPED KOMANDER IS INSPIRIT-ING YOU!

CHAPTER 168: CARRIED AWAY YO-KAI DEADCOOL

YEAH! YEAH! YEAH! ♪

OKAY! ♪

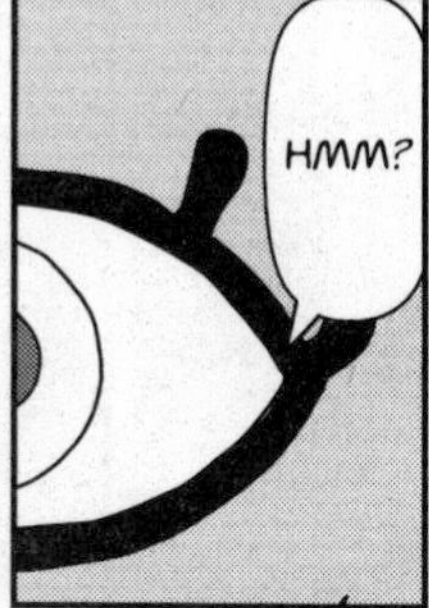

E BEST FRESH FISH
E FISH PLACE
THUNGKT
HUUURGH!
...
TWCH TWCH...
I LOST... AGAIN...
HEY, ARE YOU ALL RIGHT?
YOU MUST BE NUTS, TRYING TO FIGHT A TRUCK!
...
PEOPLE... ALWAYS TELL ME THAT...
BUT I HAVE TO DO IT...NO MATTER WHAT...!
...
WOW. MUST BE SOME KIND OF STORY BEHIND IT. I HAD NO IDEA!

I'M SORRY! ♪
CARRIED AWAY YO-KAI DEADCOOL
KRRRKT...
THUNGK
UUUNGH!
...
BOW
I'M SORRY. I GOT CARRIED AWAY...

I'M SO SORRY!
UUUNGH!
THUNGK

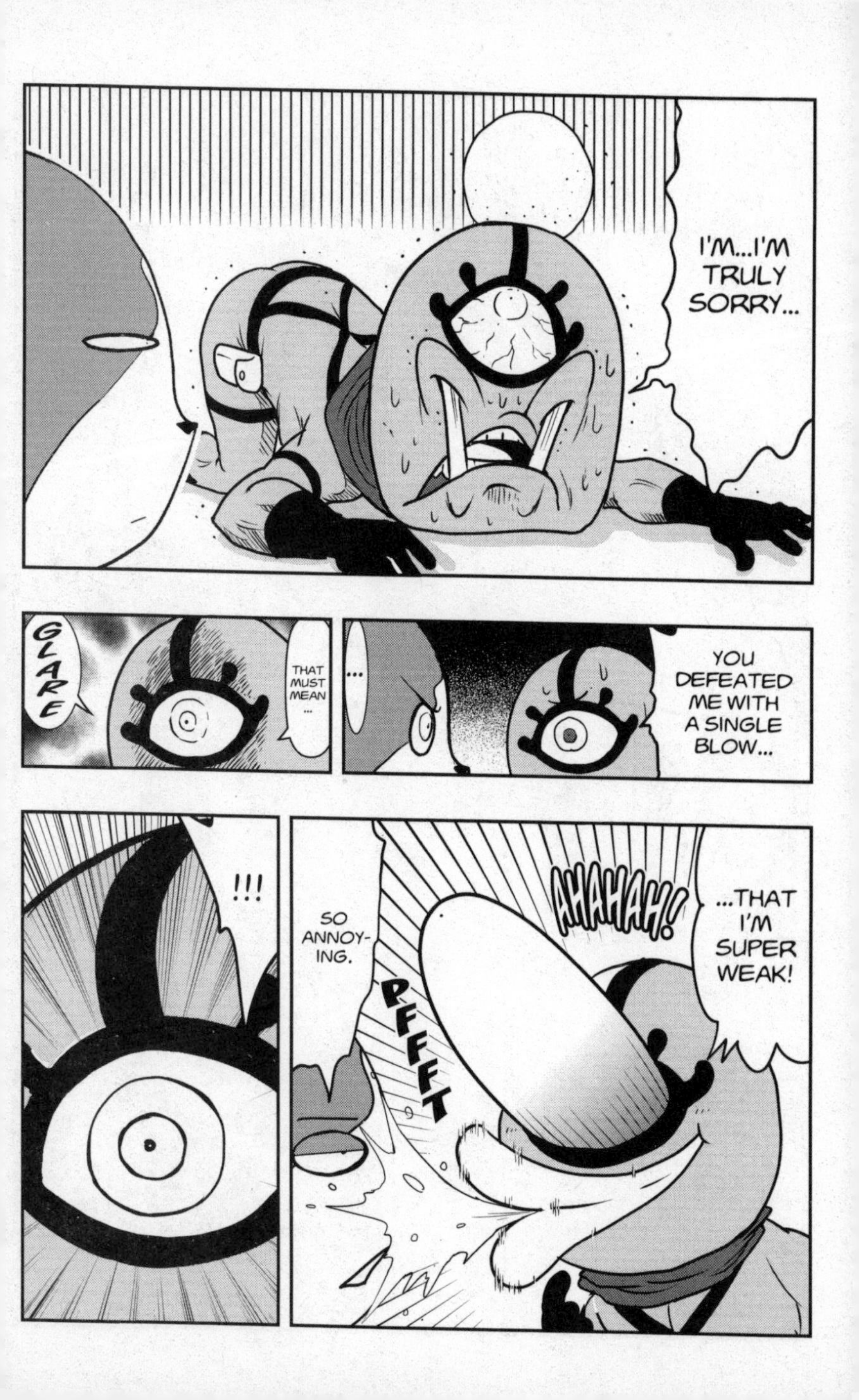
I'M...I'M TRULY SORRY...
YOU DEFEATED ME WITH A SINGLE BLOW...
...
THAT MUST MEAN ...
GLARE
...THAT I'M SUPER WEAK!
AHAHAH!
PFFFT
SO ANNOY-ING.
!!!

I HATE ANNOYING GUYS TOO. ♪
WHAT'S THAT?! WHO'S ANNOYING? TELL ME! WHO IS IT? TELL ME WHO IT IS!
TELL ME! TELL ME! TELL ME!
JUST SCRAM, WOULD YOU?!
PAPT
!!!
YOU THOUGHT I WAS WEAK AND GOT CARRIED AWAY, DIDN'T YOU?

WHEN YOU GET CARRIED AWAY EASILY, PEOPLE ALWAYS LOOK DOWN ON YOU.
GRRP...
BUT IN A FIGHT, THE MOMENT YOU LOOK DOWN ON YOUR OPPONENT YOU START LETTING YOUR GUARD DOWN...
AND THAT'S WHEN I KNOW I'VE WON!
SHA
WE'RE NOT EVEN FIGHT-ING!
OH? THEN WHY ARE YOU BACKING AWAY FROM ME?
RRRMBL...
YOU'RE SCARED, AREN'T YOU? I CAN TELL.
YOU'RE FRIGHT-ENED BECAUSE YOU HAVE NO IDEA WHAT I'M THINKING! ♪
SEE
ACTUALLY...

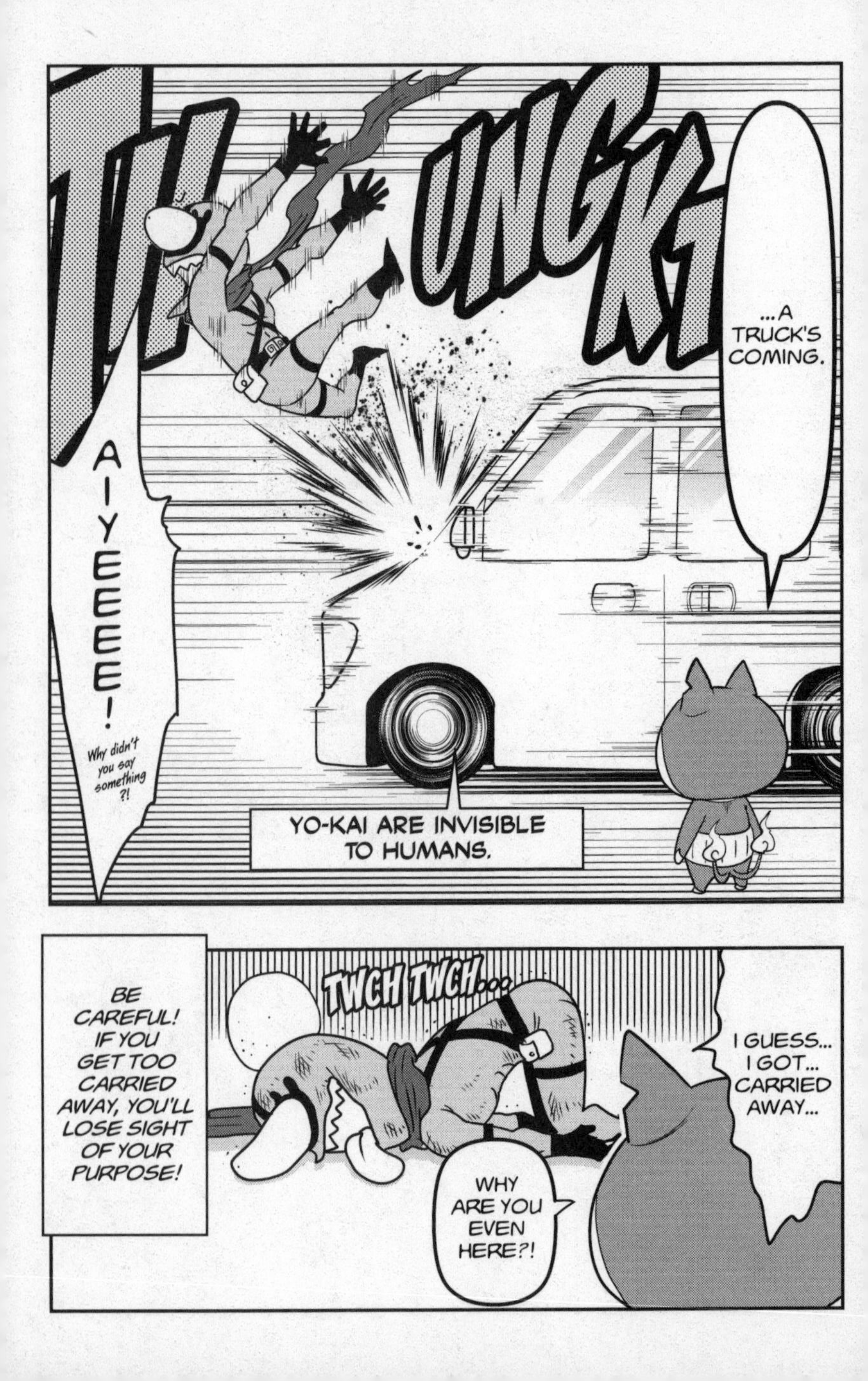
...A TRUCK'S COMING.
THUNCK!
AIYEEEEE!
Why didn't you say something?!
YO-KAI ARE INVISIBLE TO HUMANS.
BE CAREFUL! IF YOU GET TOO CARRIED AWAY, YOU'LL LOSE SIGHT OF YOUR PURPOSE!
TWCH TWCH...
I GUESS... I GOT... CARRIED AWAY...
WHY ARE YOU EVEN HERE?!

CHAPTER 169:
BACK TO BASICS
YO-KAI SHROOK

TAKE THIS! PAWS OF FURY!
VROOOO
SHF SHF SHF SHF
MEOW?
CHOOM
CHOOM
CHOOM
CAT YO-KAI JIBANYAN
SHA SHA SHA
MEEEOOOW!
SHFF SHFF
WHAT'S GOING ON?! MY PUNCHES AREN'T CONNECTING!
SHFF

VRRROOM
MEOOOW!
YO-KAI ARE INVISIBLE TO HUMANS.
ZUFF
!
WHAT'S WRONG... WITH MY PUNCHES ...?
TWCH TWCH...
WHAT... WHAT'S GOING ON?
SHUP
A SHARK! DON'T EAT ME!!!
...
THE F

VRROOM
NOOOO!
THUNCK
...
UNGH...
MEOOW! HE'S GONNA EAT ME! I'M GONNA DIE!
AHHH!
ACTU-ALLY...
YOU'RE ALREADY DEAD.
NOOOOOO!
EEEEEEK!

I HEARD ABOUT A YO-KAI...
...WHO, AFTER GETTING HIT BY A TRUCK AND TURNING INTO A YO-KAI, KEEPS COMING BACK TO FIGHT VEHICLES.
BUT YOU'RE FIGHTING WITHOUT PURPOSE!
...
BAAAAAM
YOU NEED TO GET BACK TO BASICS!
BACK TO BASICS YO-KAI SHROOK
WHAT ARE YOU TRYING TO ACCOM-PLISH?
WHY ARE YOU HERE AND WHAT ARE YOU DOING?
YOU NEED TO GET BACK TO BASICS! REMEM-BER WHAT YOU'RE FIGHTING FOR AND WHY!
...
HUH? WHERE'D HE GO?

FWAAAAA
SHWOOO
HE'S STILL FLYING UP TO THE AFTER-LIFE!
AH!
GET BACK IN THERE!
SHOVE
SHOVE
FOR CRYING OUT LOUD!
SQUEE
SQUEE

WHAT'S YOUR PROBLEM?! FIRST YOU KILL ME, NOW YOU'RE BRINGING ME BACK TO LIFE!
ACTUALLY, YOU DIED ON YOUR OWN.
?
MY NAME'S **SHROOK.**
EVEN THE GREATEST PROFESSIONAL BECOMES AN AMATEUR WHEN I INSPIRIT THEM.
A RENOWNED CHEF WON'T BE ABLE TO NAME THE SEASONING THEY'RE USING!
A CHAMPION SOCCER PLAYER WON'T EVEN BE ABLE TO KICK THE BALL!
...
SOME PEOPLE CALL IT A **SLUMP.**
*A **SLUMP** IS WHEN YOUR PERFORMANCE DECLINES AND YOU'RE UNABLE TO DO YOUR BEST.*
I RE-MEM-BER NOW!

DAAAAAA!
READ THE SERIES FROM THE BEGINNING! CHECK OUT YO-KAI WATCH VOLUME 1!
DON'T FORGET VOLUMES 2-16 TOO!
WHAT ARE YOU TALKING ABOUT?!
What does that have to do with anything?!
YO-KAI WATCH
ARE YOU THE REASON MY PUNCHES WEREN'T CONNECTING?!
I INSPIRIT PEOPLE WHO HAVE FORGOTTEN THE BASICS.
FORGOTTEN THE BASICS?! WHAT ARE YOU EVEN TALKING ABOUT?!

HOW COULD I EVER FORGET?!
IT ALL STARTED...
THAT IS...

SEVEN YEARS AGO— NO! IT WAS EIGHT!
OR MAYBE IT WAS 20...?
EHH...
HMM...
IT WAS AT AN INTER-SECTION I THINK...
I WAS HIT, OR MAYBE RUN OVER BY A TRUCK? NO! A DIFFERENT VEHICLE...?
KNOCK IT OFF! YOU DON'T REMEM-BER ANY-THING!
WHATEVER! I COULDN'T FORGIVE MYSELF FOR MAKING AMY SO SAD...
...SO I RESOLVED TO BECOME STRONG ENOUGH TO DEFEAT A TRUCK!
AND NOW SO MUCH TIME HAS PASSED...

...THAT YOU KEEP FACING OFF AGAINST VEHICLES WITH NO MEMORY OF WHY YOU'RE DOING IT!
...
YOU'RE JUST DOING THE SAME THING OVER AND OVER! ALL BECAUSE YOU FORGOT THE BASICS!
YOU'RE RIGHT...I WANTED TO BEAT THE TRUCKS...
...BUT I LOST SIGHT OF WHY I WANTED TO GROW STRONG— SO AMY WOULD BE PROUD OF ME!
VSH
THANKS FOR HELPING ME REMEM-BER!
PAWS OF...

FURY!
HUUURGH!
SHFF
SHFF
SHFF
SHFF
...
THUNCK!
I'M STILL HERE, SO YOU'RE STILL AN AMATEUR.
ENOUGH! WOULD YOU BEAT IT ALREADY?!
!
...
YOU ...

YOU FORGOT THE BASICS ONCE AGAIN! YOU NEGLECTED TO THANK ME FOR THE ADVICE I JUST GAVE YOU!
AGGH!
IF YOU WANT ME TO LEAVE, YOU'RE GONNA HAVE TO MAKE ME.
RRMBL...
I'M SO SORRY! REALLY!
MWA HA HA. NICE TRY.
I HATE INGRATES! PEOPLE WITH NO MANNERS! PEOPLE WHO DON'T KNOW HOW TO RETURN A KINDNESS!
COME ON...I DON'T WANT TO FIGHT YOU!
SHUT UP! PREPARE YOUR-SELF!

MEOOOOOW! STOP! PLEASE! I'M TRYING TO APOLOGIZE!
WHAT'S WRONG WITH YOU?! YOU THINK YOU CAN BEAT A TRUCK LIKE THIS?!
DON'T YOU WANT TO SEE THAT GIRL AGAIN?!

SH
BO
NOW, THAT WAS A GOOD PUNCH!
YOU'RE STILL AN AMATEUR THOUGH, SO IT DIDN'T HURT.
...
DID YOU...
GRIN

THE FISH PLACE
LOOKS LIKE YOU'VE FINALLY GONE BACK TO BASICS.
THIS... WAS ALL PART OF YOUR PLAN?!
GOOD LUCK WITH YOUR TRAINING! DON'T FORGET THIS FEELING!
YOUR PUNCHES WILL GO BACK TO NORMAL ONCE I'M GONE.
...
THAT'S IT!
I CAN DO THIS!
TRUUUCK!
TAKE THIS! PAWS OF FURY!
CHOOM
CHOOM
CHOOM
CHOOM
CHOOM
CHOOM
CHOOM
HUUURGH!

GOING BACK TO BASICS ISN'T THE SAME THING AS BE-COMING STRONG.

YOU CAN'T FORGET THE BASICS, BUT YOU ALSO HAVE TO TRAIN HARD!

I...I SEE...

IF YOU CAN'T DO WHAT YOU'RE NORMALLY ABLE TO, YOU MAY HAVE BEEN INSPIRITED BY SHROOK!

CHAPTER 170: SELF-DISGUST YO-KAI DISLIKING

WE'RE DECIDING WHETHER THIS CHAPTER SHOULD BE A DIRTY JOKE OR A PARODY!
LET'S DO A DIRTY JOKE!
NO! PARODIES ARE EASIER TO UNDER-STAND!
PLUS, DIRTY JOKES MIGHT OFFEND SOME PEOPLE!
PARODIES ARE JUST A DIRTY WAY TO MAKE A JOKE OF OTHER PEOPLE'S WORK!
NATE! WHO HAS THE BEST IDEA?!
YOU CHOOSE, NATE! DIRTY JOKE OR PARODY!
WELL ...

I'VE SEEN PLENTY OF BOTH IN OTHER MANGA, SO I DON'T THINK WE REALLY NEED EITHER.

HE'S RIGHT... ANYBODY CAN GET CHEAP LAUGHS WITH A PARODY.
I WAS A FOOL TO EVEN SUGGEST IT...
?
THE SAME'S TRUE FOR DIRTY JOKES...
I'M AN IDIOT...
THAT'S IT. THERE MUST BE SOME KIND OF REGRET YO-KAI NEARBY.
WAITAMINUTE! HOW COULD YOU SEE SOMEONE IN SUCH DEEP REGRET AND SAY IT'S JUST A YO-KAI?!
IT'S SO INCREDIBLY RUDE! OUR REGRET IS TRUE AND SINCERE!
LOOK...A YO-KAI.
...

SO THIS IS ALL **YOUR** FAULT!
...
HOW DARE YOU WASTE OUR TIME BY MAKING US REGRET THINGS!
HE WAS JUST SAYING HIS REGRET IS TRUE AND SINCERE...
I'M SORRY. I FEEL QUITE BAD FOR MAKING YOU FEEL BAD ABOUT YOURSELVES.
YOU MAY FORGIVE ME NOW.
YOU'RE SHOWING REGRET, BUT YOU'RE SO POMPOUS ABOUT IT!
WHO ARE YOU?

TA-DAAH!
I AM SELF-DISGUST YO-KAI, DisliKing!
SELF-DISGUST...
...IS WHEN YOU FEEL TERRIBLE ABOUT SOMETHING YOU'VE DONE AND BLAME YOURSELF.
WHERE DID YOU COME FROM? WHAT DO YOU WANT?
OFTENTIMES I FEEL BAD ABOUT MYSELF BECAUSE OF MY POWER, BUT...
I ALWAYS CHEER UP WHEN I SEE SOMEONE ELSE FEELING BAD ABOUT THEMSELVES! ♪
THANKS A LOT! WOOOHOOO!
YOU'RE AWFUL.
AWFUL?

IT'S TRUE... I'M SUCH AN AWFUL GUY.
GLOOOM
THIS GUY'S THE WORST!
I KNOW WHO WE NEED!
CALLING ...
... HAPPIERRE!
HAPPY. ♪
HAPPINESS YO-KAI HAPPIERRE
A YO-KAI THAT MAKES EVERYONE FEEL KIND AND HAPPY.

CHA CHA
CHA CHA CHA CHA♪
CHA CHA
CHA CHA CHA CHA♪
CHA CHA CHA♪
HAPPY.♪
BAAAM
HAPPY...
GLOOM
WHAT A HAPPY-LOOKING YO-KAI...
COMPARED TO HIM, MY POWER IS SO MISERABLE.
I'M...

THUNGKT
HEY !!!
HUUURGH!
I GOT SICK OF ALL HIS MOPING AROUND.
YOU CAN'T GO RIGHT TO VIOLENCE THOUGH!
Are you okay?
TWCH TWCH
YOU'RE RIGHT... I'M AN AWFUL GUY.
GLOOM
LOOK! THEY'RE COMFORTING EACH OTHER!

BWA HA HA! THANKS A BUNCH! WOOOHOOO!
SEEING SOMEONE FEEL BAD ABOUT THEM-SELVES MAKES ME FEEL GREAT!
AGAIN?! THIS IS JUST AWFUL!
...
ISN'T THERE ANYTHING YOU LIKE ABOUT YOURSELF?
AWFUL, AGAIN...
GLOOM
THIS GUY IS THE MOST ANNOYING YO-KAI I'VE SEEN IN AGES...

...
YOU'RE RIGHT. I SHOULDN'T GET OVER-WHELMED BY MY SELF-DISGUST...
EXACTLY!

...BECAUSE I KNOW I'LL FEEL BETTER WHEN I SEE MISERABLE PEOPLE! DEPRESSED PEOPLE ALWAYS BRIGHTEN MY DAY! ♪
YOUR MISERY SAVES ME!
FWAAAAAA
NO! THAT'S EXACTLY THE THING WE'RE SAYING IS SO AWFUL!
...
GLOOOM
I'LL NEVER GET PAST THIS...
I TOLD THEM WHAT I LIKED ABOUT MYSELF AND THEY SAID IT WAS AWFUL...
I KNOW! MAYBE WE CAN HELP HIM THINK MORE POSITIVELY?
I DON'T REMEM-BER ANY POSITIVE YO-KAI.
NO NO, I'M TALKING ABOUT SOMEONE ELSE. YOU KNOW... THAT YO-KAI. ♪

AAH! THAT'S RIGHT. ♪
IF NEGATIBUZZ SUCKS UP SOMEONE'S NEGATIVE FEELINGS, THEY WILL BECOME POSITIVE. ♪
THUNG
THOSE NEGATIVE FEELINGS ARE MINE!
VOOSH
HUH?
GULP GULP
SLURP SLURP
NNNGH...
NEGATIBUZZ!
I CAN ALWAYS LOOK FOR SOMEONE ELSE TO FEED OFF OF! ♪
I SHOULD CALL MYSELF THE BUMBLING BUZZ...
DRAT!
YES...I'D NEVER THOUGHT OF IT BEFORE...
THANK YOU FOR MAKING ME UNDERSTAND. ♪
CHECK OUT VOLUME 1!
!
...DON'T THINK THAT'S NECES-SARY.
I...
THAT'S IT, NATE! CALL NEGATI-BUZZ!
...
IT'S A LOT BETTER THAN SOMEONE WHO DOESN'T EVEN REALIZE THEIR FLAWS AND JUST COMPLAINS ABOUT OTHER PEOPLE. ♪
HE'S JUST A LITTLE OB-SESSED WITH IT ALL.
SO HE MUST BE PRETTY LEVEL-HEAD-ED.
HE KNOWS WHAT HIS BAD TRAITS ARE.

?

PEOPLE ALWAYS SAY I'M DEPRESS-ING, BORING AND ANNOYING...

YOU ...

!

OH!

YOU'RE OKAY.

THIS IS THE FIRST TIME SOMEONE'S ACCEPTED ME!

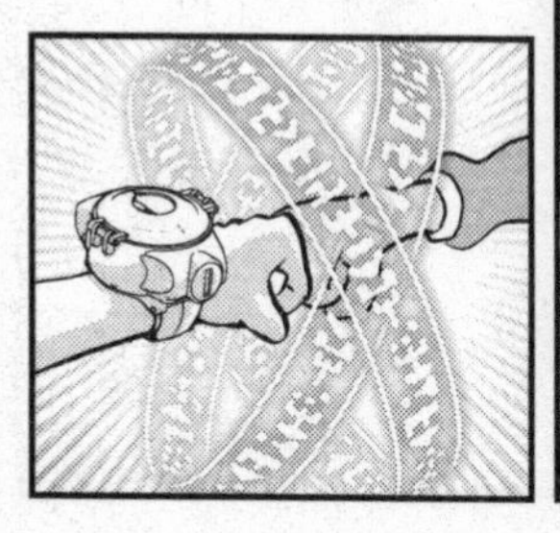

I GOT ANOTHER YO-KAI KEYSTONE! ♪
POOPT

WE WERE SO FOOLISH TO TRY AND FORCE HIM TO CHANGE WHO HE IS...
...

ARE YOU TWO DEPRESSED?
YES.
MEOW.
!
GLOOOM
WE'RE... AWFUL...
MEOW.

WOOOHOOOOO!
YEAH! ♪ I FEEL GREAT NOW!
HE CHEERS UP WHEN HE SEES PEOPLE FEELING DEPRESSED.

HUUURGH!
HE RUINED IT...
YOU SHOULD TRY TO TONE THAT DOWN SOME.
YOU... MIGHT BE RIGHT...
BE NICE TO PEOPLE WHO ARE DEPRESSED!
NATE ADAMS'S CURRENT NUMBER OF YO-KAI FRIENDS: 80

CHAPTER 171: MUSTY ATMOSPHERE YO-KAI SUNK'NSOUL

FWOO
FWOO
FWOO
FWOO
...

WHISPER, I DON'T KNOW WHY, BUT...
...I'M SICK AND TIRED OF EVERY-THING AND DON'T FEEL LIKE DOING ANY-THING.
FWOO
FWOO
FWOO
FWOO
HMM, TRY THE YO-KAI WATCH!
Behind you! Check behind you, Nate!
DON'T YOU REAL-IZE I'M NOT IN THE MOOD?
FWOO
FWOO
FWOO
FWOO
DON'T YOU REALIZE THAT THE ONE RESPON-SIBLE IS RIGHT BEHIND YOU?!

...
...
FWOO
FWOO
FWOO
FWOO
HE'S BEEN COMPLETELY INSPIRITED...
FWOO
FWOO
FWOO
FWOO
I HAVE NO OTHER CHOICE! I'LL DRIVE THE YO-KAI AWAY MYSELF!
BEGONE, YO-KAI! AND DON'T COME NEAR MY MASTER AGAIN!

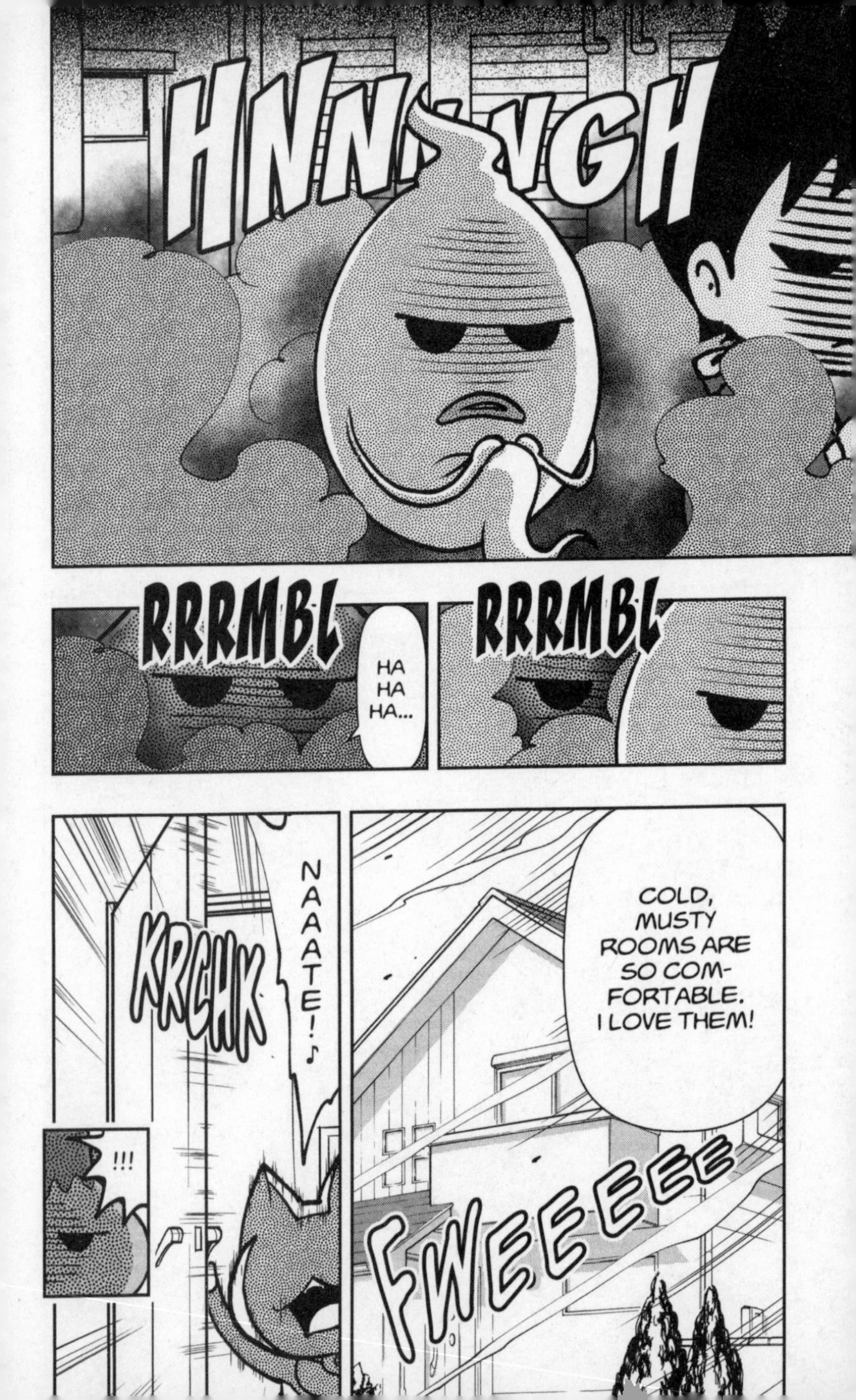
HNNNNGH
RRRMBL
HA
HA
HA...
RRRMBL
COLD, MUSTY ROOMS ARE SO COM-FORTABLE. I LOVE THEM!
FWEEEEEE
NAAAATE!♪
KRCHK
!!!

SHUDDER
SHUDDER
SHUDDER
SHUDDER
IT'S FREEZING OUTSIDE! LET ME WARM UP INSIDE!
SHUDDER
SHUDDER
SHUDDER

MEOW...
A YO-KAI! IT MUST BE!
!
HOW COULD YOU DO THIS ?!

HOW CAN NATE AND WHISPER LAUGH AND BE ENTERTAINED BY ME IF THEY'RE LIKE THIS?!
SHOOCK
THAT'S WHAT YOU'RE ANGRY ABOUT?!
WHICH YO-KAI ARE YOU? CLEARLY NOT A VERY POPULAR ONE.
!!!
YOU'RE RIGHT...
FWOO
FWOO
FWOO
FWOO
I BET THIS HAS SOME-THING TO DO WITH THAT SMOKE!
MUSTY ATMOSPHERE YO-KAI
SUNK'NSOUL
HEY, NATE! WAKE UP!
LEAVE ME ALONE ...
...

ARE YOU OKAY?
HNNRGH
HUH...?
AH! JIBANYAN?! WHAT HAPPENED?!
YOU WERE BEING INSPIRITED BY A YO-KAI!
REALLY?! WHAT YO-KAI IS IT?!
FWAASH
...
A YO-KAI THAT MAKES THE AREA AROUND YOU MUSTY.
...
NO, THAT'D BE THE SAME AS DISMARELDA!
THIS YO-KAI MUST HAVE SOME OTHER POWER!
OTHERWISE, I CAN'T EXPLAIN HOW I GOT SO BEAT-UP!
THUNGKT THUNGKT
WHISPER! WAKE UP, WILL YOU?!
...

UGH!
HUURGH
YOU FINALLY WOKE UP! YOU WERE BEING INSPIRITED BY A YO-KAI.
SO IT WAS YOU...!
THAT'S SUNK'N-SOUL!
ANYONE WHO BREATHES IN THEIR GAS GETS OVERCOME WITH A MUSTY FEELING!
BAAM
YOU MADE US FEEL MUSTY AND THEN YOU ATTACKED US! WHAT A CHEAP TRICK!
...
IT'S THE GAS!
WE JUST NEED TO OPEN THE WINDOW AND AIR OUT THE ROOM!

FWOO
FWOO
NOT SO FAST.
!!!
FWOO
FWOO
FWOO
PEEEW!
WHISPER! PLEASE... THE WINDOW ...
KOFF
KOFF
KOFF
I CAN'T! TOO MUCH... GAS...!
!
YOU'RE OUR ONLY HOPE ...!
I KNOW YOU CAN DO IT!
OKAY...I'LL GIVE IT A TRY... FOR YOU, JIBANYAN!
OKAY, GET READY!
GRAB
?!

GOOOOO!
BOOSH
WHAAAA!
KRSHAA
FWEEEE
JIBAN-YAAAAAAN!
!!!
SHWOOO
OH NO!
GOTCHA!

IT'S SO COLD! CLOSE THE WINDOW, NATE!
SHWOOO
I CAN'T... BECAUSE YOU BROKE IT.
SHUDDER
SHUDDER
SHUDDER
QUICKLY! IT'S GOING TO START SPURTING OUT GAS AGAIN!
...
BRR
BRR
COLD...
BRR
YOU TOO ?!
PAWS OF FURY!
SHUDDER
SHUDDER
THE COLD GOT TO HIM...
TRRMBLE TRRMBLE
FWIP FWIP

TWCH TWCH...
BUT JIBANYAN STILL WON! THIS GUY MUST BE REALLY WEAK...
I'M NO GOOD AT TALKING TO PEOPLE. I FIGURED I WOULDN'T HAVE TO TALK TO ANYONE IF THEY WERE ALL LIKE ME...
THAT'S REALLY SELFISH.
FWOO
FWOO
FWOO
BUT NO ONE EVER WANTED TO BECOME FRIENDS WITH ME...
...
LOOKS LIKE THE GAS COMES OUT WHEN HE'S WORRIED...
WE'LL NEVER GET NEAR HIM AT THIS RATE.
IF YOU WANT TO MAKE FRIENDS, YOU HAVE TO TAKE THE FIRST STEP. ♪
!
ZUFF
NATE! THE GAS IS GOING TO GET YOU AGAIN!

BAAAM
LET'S BE FRIENDS.
...
HEY...
A gas mask?! Where did that come from?!
...
PFFT
HA HA HA... YOU'RE A FUNNY GUY.
I'VE NEVER MET SOME-ONE LIKE YOU!
...
IT'S NICE TO MEET YOU!
THANK YOU! ♪

I GOT ANOTHER YO-KAI KEYSTONE! ♪
POP
PT
WAITA-MINUTE... WHERE'S WHISPER ...?
!
...
OH.
WHISPER, YOU SAVED THE DAY! ♪
SHWAK
REALLY? THAT'S GREAT.

JUST ONE THING LEFT TO DO...
SPLUB
PLIP PLIP
KRRK KRRK
YOU KNOW... WE DIDN'T NEED TO BREAK THAT WINDOW...
TWCH TWCH
IT FEELS A LITTLE MUSTY IN HERE AGAIN ...
IT'S NOT MY FAULT, IS IT...?
DON'T FORGET TO AIR OUT YOUR ROOM EVEN IF IT'S COLD!
NATE ADAMS'S CURRENT NUMBER OF YO-KAI FRIENDS: 81

CHAPTER 172:
INSECURE YO-KAI
RUNSURE

I'M NATE ADAMS. AN ORDINARY ELEMENTARY SCHOOL STUDENT.
GASP
GASP
WHAT'S GOING ON? I SUDDENLY FELT LIKE RUNNING AND HAVEN'T STOPPED SINCE!
WHAT AM I RUNNING FOR? I DON'T WANT TO STOP...
...
STAGGER...
...

AND THIS IS WHISPER.
A YO-KAI WHO THINKS HE'S MY BUTLER FOR SOME REASON.
WHISPER, WHAT'S UP? WHY AREN'T YOU SAYING ANYTHING?
WHAT? WELL, UMM...
...THERE'S A REASON BEHIND EVERY-THING.
YOU SEE, NATE...
?
GUESS I HAVE TO REPEAT MYSELF AGAIN...
WHICH YO-KAI IS IT NOW?
FWAAASH
ALL THE STRANGE STUFF THAT HAPPENS IN THIS WORLD... MOST OF IT IS THE DOINGS OF...
YOU FINISH IT!
I KNOW, I KNOW. YO-KAI!
EXACTLY!
HE'S SO ANNOY-ING!

SILENCE
IT RAN PAST YOU WHILE YOU WERE THINKING, "HE'S SO ANNOYING."
I DON'T SEE ANYTHING ...
SIGH
HOW MANY TIMES HAVE WE BEEN THROUGH THIS?
WHAT?! WHY DIDN'T YOU LOOK FOR ONE?!
WHY DIDN'T YOU TELL ME THERE WAS A YO-KAI HERE?!
HE'S NOT EVEN LISTENING...
IT MUST BE NEKIDSPEED!
I WAS FORCED TO RUN FOR NO REASON ...
...THEN THE YO-KAI RUSHED OFF BEFORE I COULD SPOT THEM...

I KNOW! I'LL BEFRIEND HIM...
THEN I CAN GET HIS HELP IN GYM CLASS AND ON FIELD DAY!
DASH...
...
I SEE HIM! ♪
TMP TMP TMP...
BEAT IT! DON'T INTERRUPT MY TRAINING!
MAYBE HE'S AN INTENSE JOCK YO-KAI!
I HOPE I'LL BE OKAY...
GULP...
TMP TMP...
E-EX-CUSE ME...
!

WHAT? WHO IS IT?
WHAT'S WITH THIS GUY? WHAT'S WRONG WITH HIS BODY?
TMP TMP TMP
SORRY! MY EYES ARE ON THE SIDE, SO IT'S DIFFICULT TO SEE YOU.
...
HAVE YOU SEEN A YO-KAI RUNNING AROUND HERE?
RUN-NING...? YO-KAI...?

DID I SEE ANYTHING?
WHAT? YOU'RE UNSURE?
HMMM... I'M UNSURE ABOUT THAT.
WAIT... ARE YOU THE YO-KAI THAT WAS MAKING ME RUN?!
WHICH YO-KAI ARE YOU?
...
HA HA HA ... WHICH YO-KAI AM I?!
HAR HAR HAR HAR ...
RRMBLL

HNNGH
I'M UNSURE ABOUT THAT.
Which Yo-kai am I...?
NOT A VERY BRIGHT ONE, APPARENTLY.
ARE YOU CALLING ME STUPID?! I JUST DON'T KNOW WHAT KIND OF YO-KAI I AM! THAT'S ALL!
EXACTLY... THAT'S NOT VERY BRIGHT.
WHY WERE YOU RUN-NING?
WHAT?

WHAT? WHO WAS RUN-NING?
ARRRRGH! SO... IRRITATING!
...
IRRI... TATING?
WHAT'S GOING ON?! WHAT HAPPENED ?!
JUST CALM DOWN! YOU CAN TELL ME!

KRA-
BOOM
WHOA... WHAT'S GOING ON? WHAT A WEIRDO ...
...
I'LL JUST LEAVE HIM BE.
FWAAAA
...
NATE, DID YOU SEE HIM? IT'S **THE YO-KAI RUNSURE!**
HUH? WHAT'S WRONG?
HMM... I'M UNSURE.

HEY! THERE YOU ARE! I FIGURED IT OUT! ♪
TMP TMP TMP
OH.
I KNOW WHAT KIND OF YO-KAI I AM! ♪
REALLY? WHAT KIND OF YO-KAI ARE YOU?
...
HUH?
SHOOCK
WHAT ARE YOU DOING HERE?!
I JUST LEFT YOU A MINUTE AGO!
WHAAAT?!
WHAT?! YOU'RE THE ONE WHO CAME BACK HERE!
TCH TCH TCH TCH
INSECURE YO-KAI RUNSURE
WHAT? ME? WHY?!
FORGET IT! WHAT KIND OF YO-KAI ARE YOU?!
!!!

WHAT KIND OF YO-KAI AM I...? I'M... UNSURE ABOUT THAT.
THAT'S IT... CALLING ...
... JIBANYAN!
MEEEOOOW!

IT'S NOT LIKE YOU TO GET SO IRRITATED AT A YO-KAI, NATE.
HE'S RIGHT...
BEAT HIM UP!
IT'S PROBABLY JUST THE HEAT. LET ME TALK TO HIM.
LEAVE IT TO ME!
JIBANYAN, YOU'VE MATURED SO MUCH. ♪

HEY! WHO ARE YOU?
I'M... UNSURE.
WHERE'D YOU COME FROM?
THAT WAY...NO, THIS WAY... OVER THERE? HMM...I'M UNSURE...
WHAT KIND OF YO-KAI ARE YOU?
WHAT? WHAT YO-KAI?
OH, I SEE...
MM-HMM

EAT THIS! PAWS OF FURY!
AIYEEEEEEEE!
SHOOOCK
JIBANYAN BEAT HIM SO QUICKLY!
I DON'T WANT TO BE RUDE, BUT I DON'T REALLY WANT TO BEFRIEND HIM...
AS A MATTER OF FACT, I JUST WANT TO FORGET HIM...
ME TOO. JUST THINKING ABOUT HIM IRRITATES ME.

HELP ME OUT, WAZ-ZAT?
ME TOO!
AGAIN ...?
AGAIN?
MEMORY EATING YO-KAI WAZZAT
...
HEEZE
GASP.
HEEZE
GASP.
...
TMP TMP TMP
WHY AM I RUN-NING ...?
THIS IS THE FIFTH TIME WE'VE GONE THROUGH THIS...
GO BACK TO PAGE 102!
NOW THEY BOTH FORGOT WHAT HAPPENED...

YO-KAI
WATCH
TM

CHAPTER 173:
LOOKING UP AT
THE SAME SKY
PART 1

ORDINARY ELEMENTARY SCHOOL STUDENT NATE ADAMS
IT'S SUMMER-TIME!! LET'S GO CATCH SOME BUGS!
WOO-HOO! ♪
CATCHING BUGS WITH A BUTTERFLY NET IS FOR BEGINNERS.
HOW AM I SUPPOSED TO CATCH THEM?
YOU AREN'T JUST HUNTING BUGS, NATE! THIS IS A SERIOUS BATTLE!
WE HAVE TO CATCH THEM USING OUR BARE HANDS! WITH NO TOOLS!
LOOK! A GIANT STAG BEETLE!
SHA
LEAVE IT TO ME!
I'M COUNTING ON YOU, JIBANYAN!

PAWS OF FURY! EAT THIS, GIANT STAG BEETLE!
WAIT! YOU'RE GOING TO SQUISH IT!
CHOMP
ARRRGH! IT BIT ME!
THAT FAST ?!
GUYS! YOU JUST NEED TO KICK THE TREE TO KNOCK THE BUG OFF!
BUZZ
THEN YOU CAN CATCH IT EASILY!
HIII-YAAAH!
LEAVE IT TO ME! WHISPER KIIIIICK!
CAT YO-KAI JIBANYAN

FWIP FWIP...
ARRRRGH!
I FORGOT I DON'T HAVE LEGS!
HOW COULD YOU FORGET THAT?
BUTLER YO-KAI WHISPER
MAYBE WE SHOULD STICK WITH OUR BUTTER-FLY NET.
HUH?

W-WHAT ...?

DASH
OVER HERE! THERE ARE TONS OF RHINOCEROS AND STAG BEETLES ON THIS ISLAND! ♪

HURRY, GUSTO!
I'M NOT REALLY INTO RHINOCEROS BEETLES.
TMP TMP TMP TMP
OH NO...
IT'S NOT FOR YOU! YOU'LL NEED IT WHEN YOU GO BACK TO THE YO-KAI REALM.
A RHINOC-EROS BEETLE? WHAT FOR?
AS A SOUVE-NIR FOR ALISTAIR.
BUT WHY A RHINOC-EROS BEETLE?
WHAT DO YOU MEAN?!

RHINOCEROS BEETLES ARE THE BEST SOUVENIRS!
I'VE NEVER HEARD THAT BEFORE !!
IS THIS SOME HUMAN REALM TRADI-TION?!
WHAAAAA
YUP!
BOY FROM 60 YEARS AGO JACK COBBLER
THEN WE SHOULD CATCH A REALLY BIG ONE!
BAAAM
ABSOLUTELY!
CLASSIC YO-KAI GUSTO
ALISTAIR IS JACK AND GUSTO'S FRIEND WHO EVENTUALLY BECAME LORD ENMA.
ALISTAIR WILL SHED TEARS OF JOY IF YOU BRING HIM A BIG ONE! ♪
I CAN'T WAIT! ♪
HUH?
MEOW?

WHAT'S THAT ?!
LOOK AT THAT ONE! IT'S HUGE!
YEAH!
ARE YOU REALLY GETTING WORKED UP OVER A RHINOCEROS BEETLE?
I FORGET HOW YOUNG YOU ARE...

...TATE ADAMS.
YEAH.
HUH?
WHO WOULDN'T GET EXCITED ABOUT A BIG RHINOCEROS BEETLE?!
FUTURE YO-KAI WHISPER
PEOPLE SAY THAT IF YOU CAPTURE A REALLY HUGE ONE, YOU CAN RULE THE WORLD!
BAAAM
BOY FROM THE FUTURE TATE ADAMS
I'VE NEVER HEARD THAT BEFORE! IS THAT A HUMAN REALM TRADITION ?!
YUP!
I SEE.
IN THAT CASE, I'LL CATCH THAT RHINOCEROS BEETLE FOR YOU, TATE ADAMS!
THUN
CK
I SEE! YOU'RE GOING TO KICK THE TREE, KNOCKING THE BEETLE TO THE GROUND!

KRRK
...
C'MON!
YES! LET'S GO GET THE BEETLE!
HE DESTROYED THE ENTIRE TREE...
FUTURE YO-KAI JIBANYAN
HUH?
?

A DOOR...?
WHAT'S THIS THING?
WONDER IF ANYONE'S ON THE OTHER SIDE?
THOK THOK
A YO-KAI KEYSTONE?
MAYBE I'LL GIVE THIS A TRY!

NO, IT'S MY HOUSE KEY!
THAT WON'T OPEN IT!
FWEEE
IT OPENED!
IT OPENED ?!
IT OPENED!
BUT WHY ?!
WHAT'S GOING ON? I CAN'T SEE THE OTHER SIDE ...

HOW?! HOW DID IT OPEN?!
THAT'S IMPOSSIBLE!
I USED THE KEY TO MY HOUSE.
CALM DOWN, WHISPER.
BAAAM
THAT'S NOT IMPORTANT. ♪
IT'S FINE. ♪
IT'S NOT FINE! IT'S NOT FINE AT ALL!
IT COULD BE A TRAP! WHO KNOWS WHO'S BEHIND THIS!
YOU'RE OVERTHINKING THINGS, DUMDUM. HMM, I CAN'T SEE WHAT'S INSIDE.
ME NEITHER.
HE JUST CALLED ME...A DUMDUM?!
I KNOW! ♪
WHISPER!
?

GO TAKE A LOOK INSIDE. ♪
BOOSH
NOOOOO!
WHISPER!
AHHHHHH!
...
SILENCE
I SEE NOW!
THIS THING'S DANGEROUS, NATE. DON'T GO NEAR IT! LET'S GET OUT OF HERE.
SHFF
SHFF
NO, NO, NO, NO!
WHISPER!
SHUP
WHAT IS IT?
I'M GLAD YOU'RE ALL RIGHT! ♪

SHWOOOP
YOU RANG?
WHO ARE YOU ?!
WHAT?!
?
WHAT... IT CAN'T BE... IS THIS ...?!
IS THIS A DOOR... TO THE PAST?!
...
UMM...

LONG TIME NO SEE...
... NATE.
?
...
BUT HOW CAN I EXPLAIN MYSELF...? SUMMER AND TATE ADAMS SAID...
CHANGING THE PAST IN ANY WAY MAY AFFECT THE FUTURE!
...THEY HID THEIR IDENTITY WHEN THEY WENT TO THE PAST.
I SHOULD DO THE SAME THING!
BUT...

I JUST CAN'T HELP MY-SELF!
NAAAATE!
?
WHO'S THIS GUY?
Scram, weirdo.
THUNGKT
URRGH!
...

WHAT'S WITH THIS GUY...?
HE LOOKS FREAKY.
WHAT HAPPENED TO WHISPER?
TWCH TWCH...
HEY, WHIS...
!!!
!
...
ARE THEY HIS FRIENDS?!
I HOPE NOT ...
NNNGH

SHUDDER
WHO ARE YOU GUYS?!
MEOW, THAT'S OUR LINE! YOU'RE THE ONE WHO SUDDENLY APPEARED!
MEOW?
WHERE AM I? THAT TOWN LOOKS PRETTY OLD...
...
OH!

HEY, WAIT! WHAT'S THIS DOOR?!
SHUP
THAT'S NOT IMPORTANT! JIBANYAN, YOU'VE GONE TOO FAR!
DAD ...?
...
A DOOR...TO THE PAST?! WHAT'S DAD DOING HERE...?!
DAAAAAAD!!
WHO ARE YOU?!
HOW DO YOU KNOW MY NAME ?!
LONG TIME NO SEE, NATE.
NO, DON'T!
I, UHHHH... SORRY TO INTRUDE ON YOU LIKE THIS...
B-BMP B-BMP
YOU CAN'T TELL HIM THAT WE'RE FROM THE FUTURE! OR ABOUT OUR YO-KAI!
UHMM, AHHH...
DON'T YOU GET IT?! IT COULD CHANGE THE PAST, PRESENT AND FUTURE!

THUNGK
YAAAAH!
MEEEOWGH!
WHISPER, YOU'RE OKAY!
HUMPH.
...
WAIT...
WHO ARE YOU?
HEY! ISN'T THAT A YO-KAI WATCH?!
YOU'RE RIGHT...
OH, UMM...
LOOKS LIKE THERE'S A PARTY GOING ON!

GUSTO?!
A LEGENDARY CLASSIC YO-KAI!!
!
WHAA?!
HEHEH
WHAT'S YOUR DEAL? YOU LOOK SO DIFFERENT FROM OTHER YO-KAI...
WHO ARE YOU?
UH-OH... HOW DO WE EXPLAIN?!
WE'RE PROBABLY THE ONLY ONES WHO UNDERSTAND WHAT'S GOING ON.
JIBANYAN, DON'T SAY ANYTHING YOU DON'T HAVE TO! IT'S ONLY GOING TO CAUSE...
B-A-A-A-M
I'M JIBANYAN. I'M YOU FROM THE FUTURE!
!!!
NO! IT'S JUST GOING TO FREAK HIM OUT!

I FIGURED AS MUCH! WE'VE GOT THE SAME COLORED FUR AND YOU'RE WEARING THE SAME COLLAR AND BELLY BAND AS ME! ♪
I GUESS THAT'S FUTURE WHISPER THEN! ♪
HE BELIEVED IT?!
BINGO!
THAT WAS QUICK!
IF YOU'RE FROM THE FUTURE AND WE'RE FROM THE PRESENT...
...THEY MUST BE FROM THE PAST! ♪
FUTURE
PAST
PRESENT
...
HOW'S HE TAKING THIS SO WELL?!
THE OTHERS WILL NEVER BELIEVE IT THOUGH!
WHAT SHOULD I TELL THEM...?

HMM, SO THIS IS THE FUTURE!
IT'S THE PRESENT FOR US!
AND THE PAST FOR US!
NO WONDER YOUR CLOTHES ARE SO SIMPLE... YOU'RE FROM THE PAST! ♪
OH NO, IT'S BECAUSE I'M POOR. ♪
OH! I'M SORRY!
YOU'RE WHISPER? FREAKY.
HAVE YOU SEEN *YOUR* FUTURE SELF?!
THEY'RE... ALL FINE WITH IT?!
JIBAN-YAN...
PSST
PSST
DO YOU REALLY BELIEVE THEY'RE FUTURE VERSIONS OF YOU TWO?
JUST BECAUSE HE HAS THE SAME FUR, OUTFIT AND NAME AS ME DOESN'T MEAN WE'RE THE SAME YO-KAI.
THEN WHAT DOES THAT MEAN? THEY SEEM REALLY FAMILIAR ...
OH, THAT'S EASY...

IT'S JUST A COINCIDENCE! ♪
That's all!
BAAAM
YUP! ♪
THAT'S EVEN MORE UNLIKELY...
I WONDER WHAT THE FUTURE HOLDS?
MEOW.
THE TOWN LOOKS TOTALLY DIFFERENT.
I HOPE I'M RICH AND LIVE IN A BIG HOUSE!
WHAT'S GOING ON?! I FELT A RIFT IN THE SPACE-TIME CONTINUUM...
SHUP...
!
...BUT I NEVER THOUGHT THIS DOOR WOULD BRING ME HERE!
SOMEONE ELSE HAS COME THROUGH!

HOVERNYAN!!!
GREETINGS! TRAVELING THROUGH TIME AND SPACE IS USUALLY A HARD THING FOR PEOPLE TO ACCEPT...
...BUT I GUESS ONCE YOU'VE USED A YO-KAI WATCH, IT'S NOT THAT DIFFICULT TO WRAP YOUR BRAIN AROUND!

YUP!
YOU'RE RIGHT!
I'VE EVEN TRAVELED TO THE YO-KAI REALM!
YES, BUT WHAT'S BROUGHT YOU ALL TOGETHER...
...THIS DOOR ITSELF, IS THE PROBLEM.
HUH?
NATE, WHAT'S THAT ON THE GROUND?
!
THERE'S SOMETHING WRITTEN ON IT.
WHAT IS IT? DON'T TELL ME IT'S INSTRUCTIONS FOR THE DOOR.
WHAT...?!

HEY, NATE! HOW'S IT GOING?
I MADE AN EXPERIMENTAL DOOR THAT LETS YOU TRAVEL TO THE PAST AND FUTURE. PLEASE TEST IT OUT FOR ME! IT'LL OPEN IF YOU PUT YOUR WATCH NEAR IT! DON'T BLAME ME IF IT DOESN'T WORK AND SOMEONE DIES.
BEST,
LORD ENMA

...
TEST IT OUT ...?
IS ALISTAIR LORD ENMA NOW?
HE'S STILL SO SILLY. ♪
MEOW. ♪
SO THERE'S NO REAL POINT TO US BEING HERE THEN.
LET'S GO HOME...

WAIT!
?
YO-KAI FROM THE PAST, PRESENT AND FUTURE HAVE ALL GATHERED HERE.
WHY DON'T WE SEE...WHICH YO-KAI IS THE STRONGEST?
!
...
...
OH, MAN ...
OOH! ♪
...
...

SOUNDS LIKE FUN!
HEH. I'VE GOT SOME TIME TO KILL.
MEOW HA HA. ♪ I'LL SHOW YOU HOW POWERFUL AN ANCIENT YO-KAI CAN BE!

DOING THIS ONE-ON-ONE WILL TAKE FOREVER! WE'LL START WITH ALL SIX AND END WITH THE WINNER!
IT'S A YO-KAI BATTLE ROYALE!
PERFECT!
I LIKE IT!
GRIN
SIX...?
...
1
2
3
4
5
6
WE HAVE TO FIGHT?!
READY?!

FIGHT!

CHAPTER 174: LOOKING UP AT THE SAME SKY PART 2

JIBANYAN!
?

URGH!
GURGH!

YOU'RE NOT BAD, FUTURE ME.
THE OLD ME AIN'T BAD EITHER.
IT'S A YO-KAI BATTLE ROYALE FROM ACROSS THE AGES!
NATE! YOU SHOULD BATTLE TO SEE WHICH OF YOU IS BEST AT USING THE...

CAN I SEE YOUR YO-KAI WATCHES? ♪
YOURS IS A LITTLE DIFFERENT FROM OURS! ♪
THEY'RE GETTING ALONG!
They aren't interested in fighting at all!
MEEOWW!

OOF...I'M NOT THE FIGHTING TYPE.
!
WE SHOULD JOIN FORCES! WHAT DO YOU SAY, JIBANYAN?
THAT'S CHEAT-ING! IT'S EVERY-ONE FOR THEM-SELVES!
THE RULE WAS LAST YO-KAI STANDING WINS. THERE WAS NOTHING ABOUT TEAMING UP!
THAT'S RIGHT!
I LIKE THAT.

BAAM
I'M IN.
HAVE YOU NO PRIDE?!
YOU JUST WANT TO WIN NO MATTER WHAT, HUH?!
WELL, IF THAT'S THE WAY YOU WANT IT...
!!!
GUSTO!

LET'S GET RID OF THE BIG GUY FIRST!
...
SHUP
LOOKS LIKE WE'RE IN TROUBLE...
HEY!
GO AHEAD. JOIN FORCES.
WE'LL TAKE YOU OUT ONE BY ONE.
RIGHT, WHIS-PER?
?
...

LOOKING FOR SOME-ONE?
WHY YOU...
SORRY, JIBANYAN, BUT I'M IN IT TO WIN IT!
GRIIIN
IT DOESN'T MATTER HOW MANY OF YOU THERE ARE! IT'S ALL...

POINTLESS,
POINTLESS,
POINTLESS,
POINTLESS,
POINTLESS,
POINTLESS,
POINTLESS,
POINTLESS,
POINTLESS,
POINTLESS,
POINTLESS,
POINTLESS,
POINTLESS,
POINTLESS,
POINTLESS,
POINTLESS,
POINTLESS,
POINTLESS,
POINTLESS,
POINTLESS!
HE'S TOO POWER-FUL!
WE NEED SOMEONE BIG TOO! HOVERNYAN—
I'M ON IT.
HEY, WHISPER.
YES?
TALK TO ME ABOUT SOME-THING.
HUH? ABOUT WHAT?
ANYTHING! JUST HURRY UP!
HMM.

WHAT DO YOU MEAN BY "ANYTHING?" I'M SUPER CAPABLE, BUT I CAN'T TALK ABOUT EVERYTHING, SO I MIGHT NOT BE ABLE TO COMPLY WITH YOUR REQUEST.
OF COURSE, AS AN EXPERIENCED BUTLER, I COULD PROBABLY DETERMINE WHAT YOU WANT FROM YOUR EXPRESSION AND BODY LANGUAGE. IT WON'T BE 100 PERCENT CORRECT, OF COURSE, BUT I'LL DO MY BEST TO HELP YOU!
AND IN THE UNLIKELY EVENT THAT I'M INCORRECT, I'D LIKE FOR YOU TO STILL GIVE ME CREDIT FOR A GOOD EFFORT. HOW DOES THAT SOUND TO YOU?
FWOOOOSH
?
WHAT?!
BLUB
BLUB
BLUB
THAT'S RIGHT! HOVERNYAN GAINS WEIGHT WHEN HE'S STRESSED!
?!
AND THEN ...

UMMPH.
...HE TURNS INTO MEGAN-YAN!
WHAT JUST HAP-PENED ...?
!!!
COOL! ♪
HE TRANS-FORMED!
WOW! WHISPER'S LONG MONOLOGUE REALLY STRESSED HOVERNYAN OUT! ♪
WHAT ARE YOU SO HAPPY ABOUT!? YOU'RE FUTURE ME, YOU KNOW?!
WELL PLAYED. BUT I JUST KNOW THAT MEGANYAN IS BIG, NOTHING MORE.
MEOW HA HA! I KNOW THAT TOO!

DROP THE BOMB!
GKT
UMMMMPH!
THUN
!!!
MEOW HA HA!♪
KRRSHAA
AGGGH!
MEGANYAN BOMB WAS A SUCCESS! I CRUSHED EVERYONE! ♪
YOU FOOL.

DID YOU THINK WE COULDN'T DODGE THAT?
...
THEN... WHAT WAS THAT "AGGGH!" ABOUT...?
FWOOO
UMMPH, THAT HURT.
PLIP PLIP...
OH NOOOO!
WHAT ARE YOU DOING?

FOR GOODNESS SAKE...
BWOOSH
HAH!
UHH...
IS HE ...?
WHAT?
MEOW HA HA HA!
RRMMBL
YOU GROW HUGE WHEN YOU'RE HIT BY MEGANYAN'S SNORT!

HUPT!
JIBANYAN BODY PRESS!
AGGGH!
DID YOU THINK YOU'D HIT ME WITH A SLOW MOVE LIKE THAT?!
HAH! YOUR PUNCHES ARE TOO PUNY TO...
CHOOOM
MY EEEEEEYE!
CHOOOM
MY OTHER EEE-EEYE!
...
MEOW, MY EYES...I CAN'T SEE...!
YOU ...

CHOOM CHOOM CHOOM CHOOM
I MIGHT BE BLIND, BUT I'M STILL HUGE! I'LL GET YOU IF I KEEP PUNCHING!
HE CAN'T SEE, SO HE'S ATTACKING EVERY-ONE!
JIBAN-YAN, STOP!
AHHHH!

THUUNGKT
NAAAAAATE!
TATE ADAMS!

JIBANYAN!
GRRR...
WOW ...!
AWESOME!! THROW HIM OUT OF THE WAY!
HEH ...

HE'S TOO HUGE!
SQUISH
JIBANYAAAAAN!

WHOA! THE FOREST'S SHAKING!
IT'S NOT JUST THE FOREST ...!

THE PLANET CRACKED IN HALF!
KRRRRRRCK

ARRRGH!
AIIII!!
JIBANYAN!
JIBANYAAAAAN!
I'M COMING!
HOVERNYAN, THOSE TWO CAN TAKE CARE OF THEMSELVES!
WE NEED TO DO SOMETHING ABOUT THE EARTH!
GOT IT!
I'LL TAKE CARE OF THIS!

ZZZZP
DUCT TAPE ?!
POINTLESS, POINTLESS, POINTLESS, POINTLESS, POINTLESS, POINTLESS, POINTLESS, POINTLESS, POINTLESS, POINTLESS, POINTLESS, POINTLESS, POINTLESS, POINTLESS, POINTLESS, POINTLESS, POINTLESS, POINTLESS, POINTLESS, POINTLESS!
THERE'S ONLY ONE WAY.
!
WHAT ARE YOU GOING TO DO?!
GUSTO AND I WILL SPLIT UP AND...
WE'LL KICK THE EARTH FROM BOTH SIDES!
KICK
STICK
SUCCESS
IT'S THAT EASY!
...

POINTLESS, POINTLESS, POINTLESS, POINTLESS, POINTLESS, POINTLESS, POINTLESS, POINTLESS, POINTLESS, POINTLESS, POINTLESS, POINTLESS, POINTLESS, POINTLESS, POINTLESS, POINTLESS, POINTLESS, POINTLESS, POINTLESS, POINTLESS!
I UNDER-STAND!
GREAT IDEA!
LET'S GO!
MEOW!
...
HERE'S THE SPOT!
LET'S DO IT!

KRA-DOOOOM
SHUUUUUUUK
...
IT WORKED ...?

WE DID IT!
MEOW! ♪
YOU TWO ARE AMAZING!
UM...
WHERE ARE THE JIBANYANS?
...

...
...
...

THEY'RE HERE
NNNGHH!!
WE FORGOT ABOUT THEM!

I'M SO SORRY.
...
WE SUMMONED THEM BACK WITH THE YO-KAI KEYSTONE.
SO ...
IT DOESN'T REALLY MATTER WHICH OF YOU IS THE STRON-GEST!
THE BEST YO-KAI IS THE ONE WHO HELPS THE MOST PEOPLE AND OTHER YO-KAI!
...
HE ALWAYS WAS GOOD AT SUMMING THINGS UP IN THE END.
HUH?

FWAAAA
THE DOOR!
IT'S STARTING TO FADE!
BUT WHY SO SUDDENLY...?!
HEY, NATE! HOW'S IT GO
I MADE AN EXPERI
DOOR THAT LETS Y
TO THE PAST AN
PLEASE TEST IT O
IT'LL OPEN IF
YOUR WATCH NE
DON'T BLAME ME
DOESN'T WORK AND
SOMEONE DIES.
BEST,
LORD ENMA
LORD ENMA SAID THE DOOR WAS **EXPERIMENTAL**, SO MAYBE THE DOOR IS STILL INCOMPLETE...?
YOU SHOULD GO BACK WHILE YOU STILL CAN!
YOU'RE RIGHT!
THIS WAS FUN! I HOPE WE MEET AGAIN SOMEDAY!
ME TOO! ♪
LET'S GO, GUSTO.
MEOW.
GOOD-BYE! ♪
...
...
?

I... UMM...
I'M GLAD I GOT TO SEE YOU AGAIN.
AGAIN?
JIBANYAN! WHISPER! LET'S GO!
YOU GOT IT.
COMING! ♪
WAIT, WHAT DO YOU MEAN BY AGAIN?
GOOD-BYE!
BYE, HOVER-NYAN!
THEY DISAP-PEARED.
IS THAT **REALLY** WHAT WE'RE GOING TO BECOME?
MEOW...
I'M NOT SURE...

DEALING WITH YO-KAI IS ALWAYS EXCITING! AND STRANGE!
YOU SAID IT.

WE CAN CATCH BUGS LATER! LET'S GO FIND SOME PEOPLE OR YO-KAI WHO NEED OUR HELP!
YEAH! ♪
MEOW. ♪
BZZZ
BZZZ

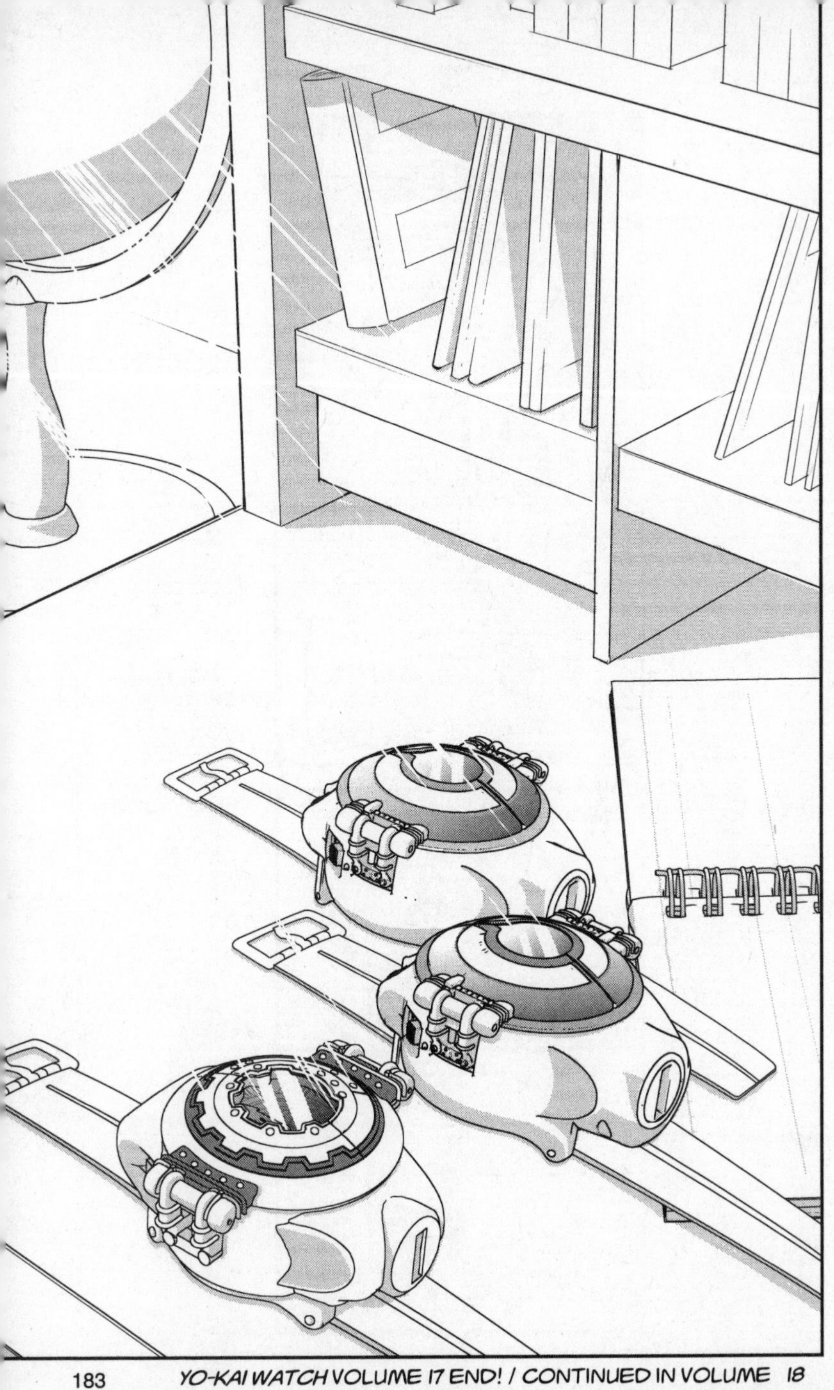

 YO-KAI WATCH VOLUME 17 END! / CONTINUED IN VOLUME 18

MAIN CHARACTER

AUTHOR BIO

The official character of my hometown,
Nagasaki Prefecture, Shimabara City, which I designed...

Guardian of Shimabara
Shimabaran

All kinds of goods have been created and are
now being sold.
Please feel free to pick one up when you see it!

Noriyuki Konishi hails from Shimabara City in Nagasaki Prefecture, Japan. He debuted with the one-shot *E-CUFF* in *Monthly Shonen Jump Original* in 1997. He is known in Japan for writing manga adaptations of *AM Driver* and *Mushiking: King of the Beetles*, along with *Saiyuki Hiro Go-Kū Den!*, *Chōhenshin Gag Gaiden!! Card Warrior Kamen Riders*, *Go-Go-Go Saiyuki: Shin Gokūden* and more. Konishi was the recipient of the 38th Kodansha manga award in 2014 and the 60th Shogakukan manga award in 2015.

Little Battlers eXperience
Story and Art by
HIDEAKI FUJII
LBX
LITTLE BATTLERS EXPERIENCE

LBX
LITTLE BATTLERS EXPERIENCE
2
Story and Art by
HIDEAKI FUJII

LBX
LITTLE BATTLERS EXPERIENCE
3
Story and Art by
HIDEAKI FUJII

LBX
LITTLE BATTLERS EXPERIENCE
4
Story and Art by
HIDEAKI FUJII

LBX
LITTLE BATTLERS EXPERIENCE
5
Story and Art by
HIDEAKI FUJII

LBX
LITTLE BATTLERS EXPERIENCE
6
Story and Art by
HIDEAKI FUJII

THIS IS THE END OF THIS GRAPHIC NOVEL!

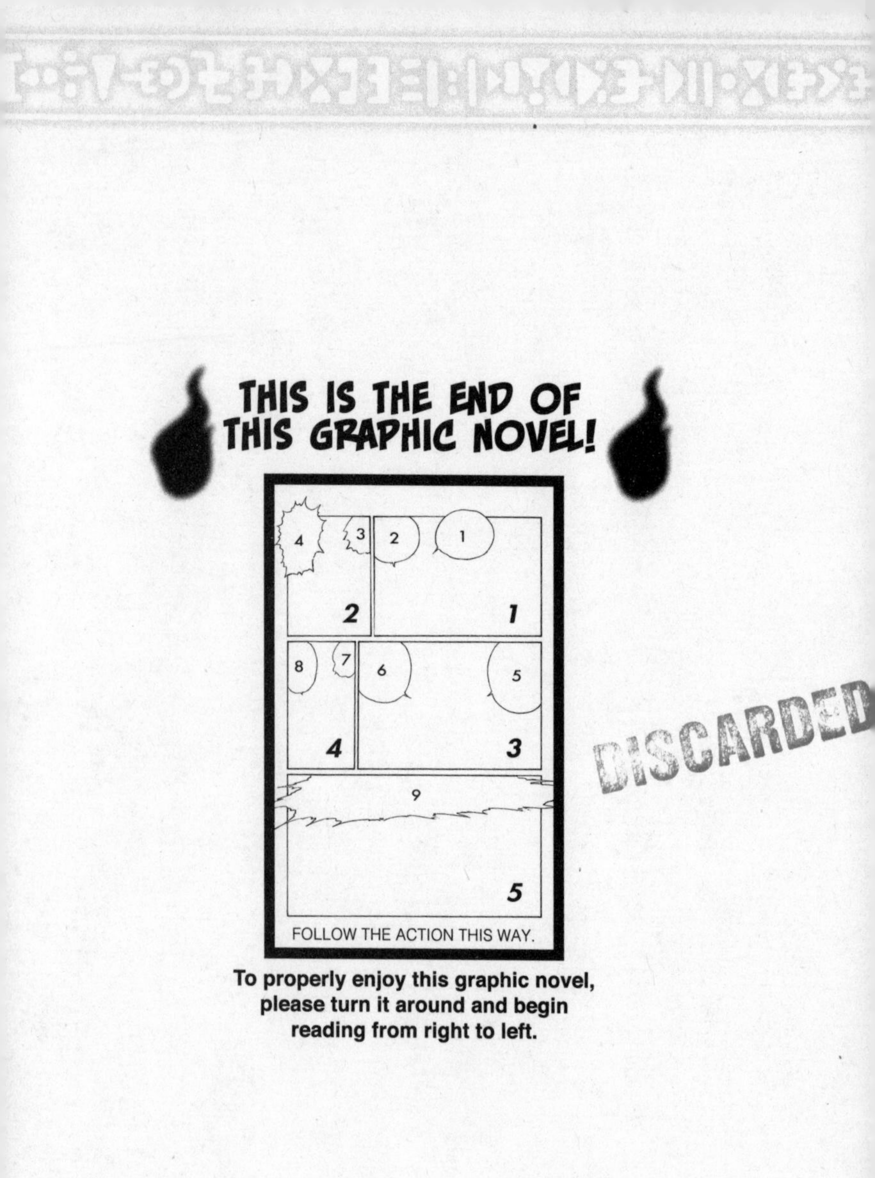
FOLLOW THE ACTION THIS WAY.

To properly enjoy this graphic novel, please turn it around and begin reading from right to left.